SAMMY SPIDER'S
FIRST
SIMCHAT TORAH

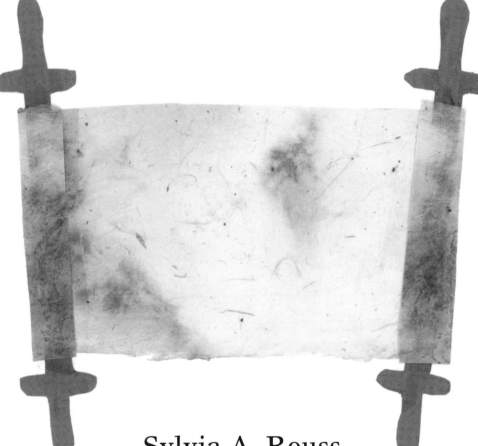

Sylvia A. Rouss

Illustrated by
Katherine Janus Kahn

KAR-BEN
PUBLISHING

To Hayden and Derek, who always find delight in the
beauty of God's creations. —S.A.R.

To my husband, David, who has stood by me in good times and
bad. I appreciate his artistic eye. —K.J.K.

Text copyright © 2010 by Sylvia A. Rouss
Illustrations copyright © 2010 by Katherine Janus Kahn

KAR-BEN PUBLISHING
A division of Lerner Publishing Group, Inc.
241 First Avenue North
Minneapolis, MN 55401 U.S.A.
1-800-4KARBEN

Website address: www.karben.com

Library of Congress Cataloging-in-Publication Data

Rouss, Sylvia A.
    Sammy Spider's first Simchat Torah/ by Sylvia A. Rouss ;
illustrated by Katherine Janus Kahn.
       p.   cm.
    Summary: Sammy Spider's mother explains to him the holiday
of Simchat Torah, when Jews eat candied apples and celebrate
the importance of reading the Torah. Includes a recipe for
candied apples.
    ISBN 978-0-7613-3965-6 (lib. bdg. : alk. paper)
    [1. Simchat Torah—Fiction. 2. Spiders—Fiction.]
    I. Kahn, Katherine, ill. II. Title.
    PZ7.R7622Saqe 2010
    [E]—dc22   2009001872

Manufactured in the United States of America
1 – DP – 7/15/10

Again

...and again

...and again

...and again

Mrs. Spider gently rocked Sammy to sleep in their web on the Shapiros' living room ceiling.

Josh was snuggled up against his mother on the couch below. "Time to put on your pajamas," Mrs. Shapiro said.

"Will you read me a story first?" Josh asked. "My teacher let me borrow the book she read in school today."

"Why don't you choose a book you haven't heard?" suggested Mrs. Shapiro.

"I really like this one," Josh insisted.

"Can you read me a story, too?" Sammy asked Mrs. Spider.

"Silly little Sammy." She hugged him. "Spiders don't read books. Spiders spin webs. But you may listen while Mrs. Shapiro reads to Josh."

Sammy lowered himself on his web to get a better look. Mrs. Shapiro opened the book and read about how God created the world with the sun, the moon, and the stars, the flowers and trees, the animals and people.

"Wow!" said Sammy as he looked at the beautiful pictures. "Mother, come see. I'm in this book," Sammy called, pointing to a picture of insects.

"Yes, Sammy, that spider does look like you," she agreed.

Mrs. Shapiro finished the story and closed the book. "Please, will you read it again?" asked Josh.

"I want to hear it too," Sammy thought.

"Maybe tomorrow," laughed Mrs. Shapiro. "It's bedtime."

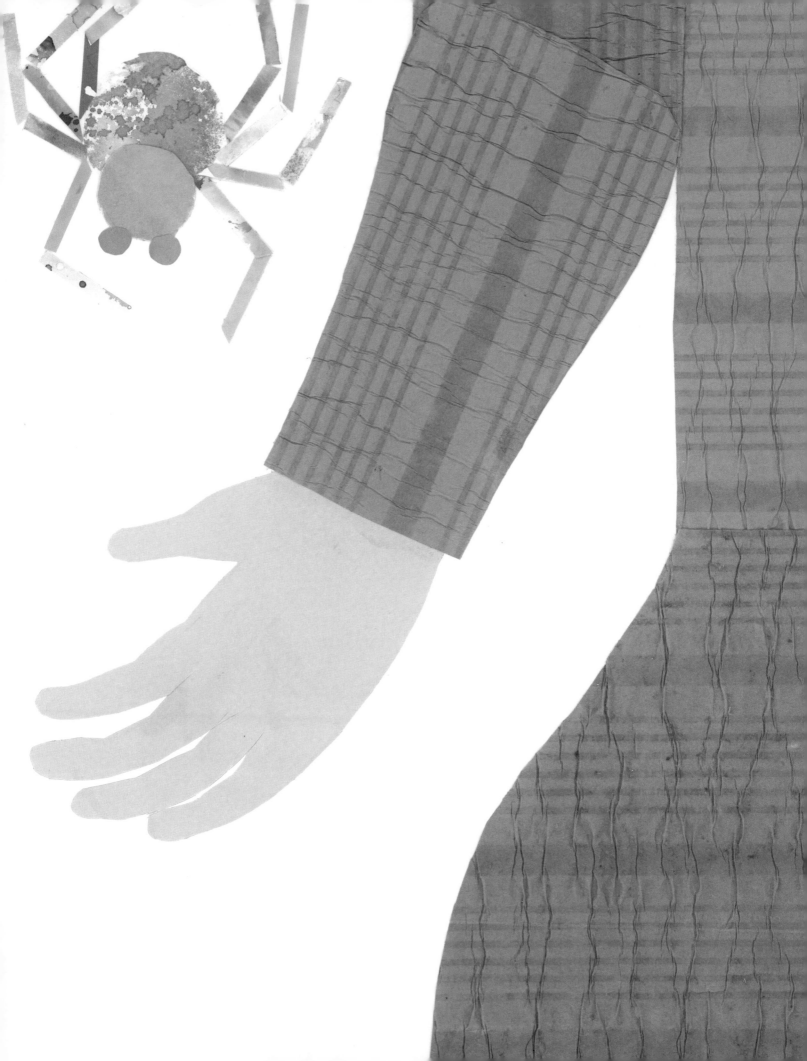

The next day, Josh dashed into the house with a small Torah scroll. "See what I made at school for Simchat Torah!" he proudly announced.

"What's Simchat Torah?" Sammy called to his mother, who was busy spinning.

"Simchat Torah is a special holiday for the Torah," she explained. "Josh will march with his little Torah at synagogue services."

"But what's a Torah?" Sammy asked as he climbed up to join his mother.

"It's a scroll that tells the story of the Jewish people. Each week on Shabbat, a part of the Torah is read in synagogue. On Simchat Torah, the congregation will finish reading it and begin all over again," Mrs. Spider responded.

"Can we celebrate with the Torah?" asked Sammy.

"Silly little Sammy. Spiders don't celebrate Simchat Torah. Spider's spin webs," replied Mrs. Spider.

Sammy watched Josh march around the house singing, "*Torah, Torah, Torah.*"

Before bedtime, Josh handed Mr. Shapiro a book. "Daddy, will you read this to me?"

"Isn't this the story your mother read to you yesterday?" asked his father.

"Yes, it's my favorite," declared Josh. "I like to hear it again and again."

The next day, Josh brought
a flag home from school.
"It's for the Simchat Torah
parade," he said.

"I know just
what your flag
needs," Mr. Shapiro
said, holding a
basket of freshly
picked apples.

Sammy watched Josh wash the apples, while Mrs. Shapiro stirred a pot of sweet syrup on the stove. When the syrup cooled, she helped Josh dip the apples into the mixture.

"What are they making?" Sammy asked.

Mrs. Spider stopped her spinning. "Those are candy apples for the Simchat Torah flags, to remind us how sweet it is to learn Torah."

"Can we make candy apples too?" Sammy asked.

"Silly little Sammy. Spiders don't celebrate Simchat Torah. Spiders spin webs," she said.

That evening, as the Shapiros got ready for Simchat Torah services, Sammy crawled down to get a closer look at the candy apples. The shiny coating felt sticky as he climbed onto the tray. He tried to move, but he was stuck.

Suddenly Josh ran into the kitchen, grabbed an apple, and put it on top of his flag. He didn't notice Sammy as he dashed out of the house to join his parents.

"I'll see you after services!"
Sammy shouted to his mother,
who was watching from above.

At the synagogue, Sammy watched the rabbi open the ark and remove all the big Torah scrolls. He handed them to Josh's parents and other adults. They paraded in a circle, singing and dancing with the Torahs. Josh and the other children joined in, carrying their little Torahs and waving their flags. Sammy giggled as he clung to the apple atop Josh's flag.

After awhile, the rabbi placed one of the Torah scrolls on the reading stand, while the others were returned to the ark. When everyone was seated, he unrolled it and read a few verses. "Tomorrow we will finish the Torah and begin to read it all over again, starting with the story of the creation of the world," he announced.

"That's my favorite story!" Josh whispered to his parents.

When the Shapiros came home, Sammy pried himself off the apple and scurried up to his web, his feet still sticky.

"The Torah is the Jewish people's favorite story," he told his mother. "That's why they like to read it again and again."

"Yes," agreed Mrs. Spider, noticing that Sammy's sticky feet had torn their web. "And you're why I have to spin our web again and again," she sighed.

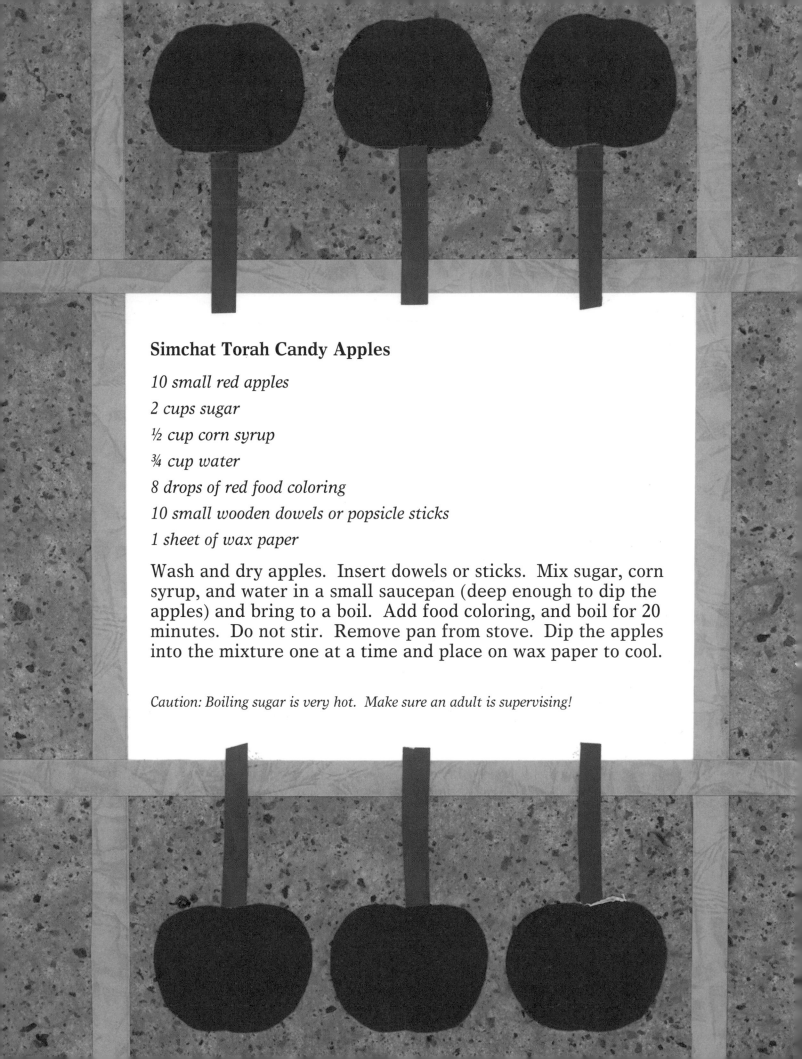

Simchat Torah Candy Apples

10 small red apples

2 cups sugar

½ cup corn syrup

¾ cup water

8 drops of red food coloring

10 small wooden dowels or popsicle sticks

1 sheet of wax paper

Wash and dry apples. Insert dowels or sticks. Mix sugar, corn syrup, and water in a small saucepan (deep enough to dip the apples) and bring to a boil. Add food coloring, and boil for 20 minutes. Do not stir. Remove pan from stove. Dip the apples into the mixture one at a time and place on wax paper to cool.

Caution: Boiling sugar is very hot. Make sure an adult is supervising!